This Ladybird Book belongs to:

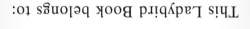

MEIKLEMILL SCHOOL
ELLON ABERDEENSHIRE

All children have a great ambition … to read by themselves.

Through traditional and popular stories, each title in the **Read It Yourself** series introduces children to the most commonly used words in the English language (*Key Words*), plus additional words necessary to tell the story.
The additional words appearing in this book are listed below.

Puss, master, boots, food, king, Marquis, Carrabas, partridges, princess, marry, clothes, carriage, working, ogre, change, lion, mouse

Ladybird books are widely available, but in case of difficulty may be ordered by post or telephone from: Ladybird Books, Cash Sales Department, Littlegate Road, Paignton, Devon. TQ3 3BE. Telephone 0803 554761.
A catalogue record for this book is available from the British Library.

Revised edition
Published by Ladybird Books Ltd Loughborough Leicestershire UK
Ladybird Books Inc Auburn Maine 04210 USA
Printed in England
© LADYBIRD BOOKS LTD MCMXCIII

Ladybird

Puss in Boots

by Fran Hunia
illustrated by Kathie Layfield

Here is Puss
with his master.

The boy has
no mummy or daddy.

He has no home.

I can help you
to get a home
says Puss.
Get me some boots,
please.

Yes, says his master.
I can get
some boots for you.

He gets Puss
some red boots.

Puss puts the boots on.

I look good in my boots,
he says.
Please get me a bag,
Master.

His master gives Puss
a bag.

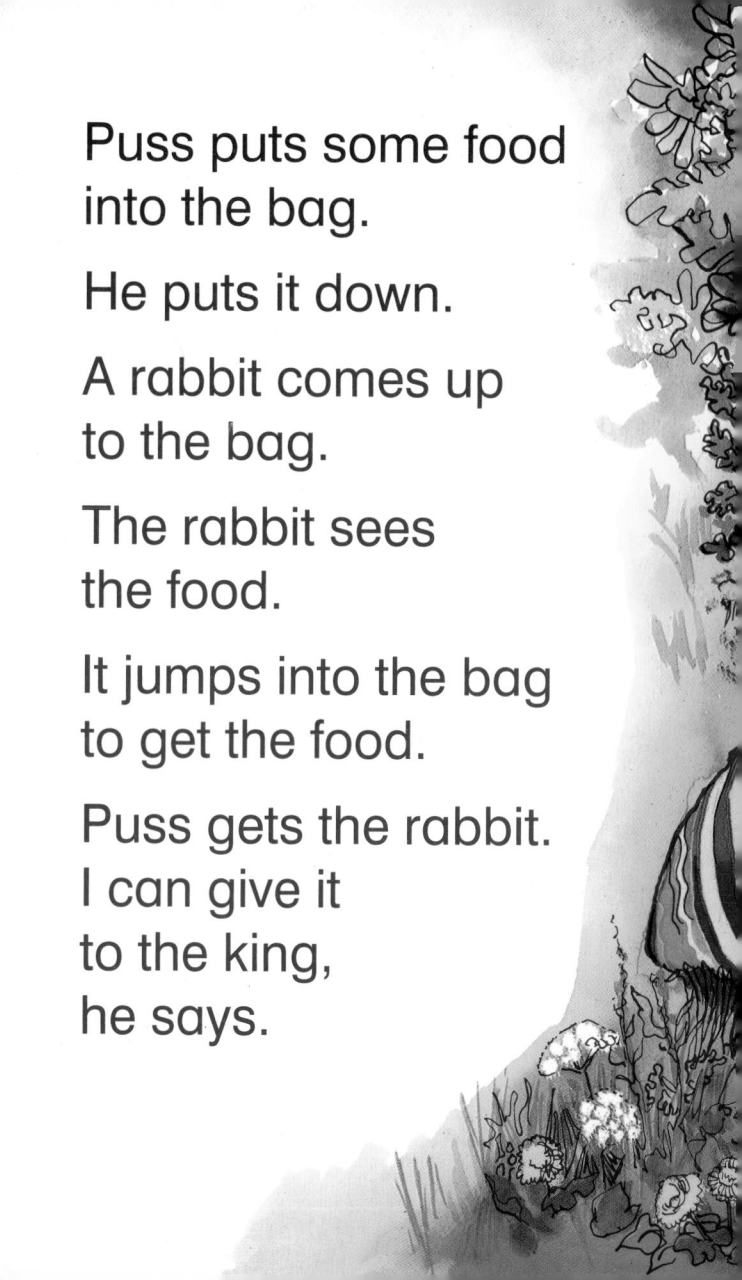

Puss puts some food
into the bag.

He puts it down.

A rabbit comes up
to the bag.

The rabbit sees
the food.

It jumps into the bag
to get the food.

Puss gets the rabbit.
I can give it
to the king,
he says.

Puss goes to the king.

This rabbit is from
my master, the Marquis
of Carrabas, he says.

The king is pleased.

He likes to eat rabbit.

Puss sees some partridges.
I can get some for the king,
he says.
He puts some food
into his bag.

The partridges want the food.

They go into the bag
to get it.

Now Puss has
the partridges.

Puss sees the king.

Here are
some partridges
for you, he says.
They are
from my master,
the Marquis of
Carrabas.

Good, says the king.
I like partridges.

Puss is up in a tree.

He sees the king
and the princess.

He comes down
and says to his master,
Here come the king
and the princess.

Come with me,
and you can marry
the princess.

Get into the water,
says Puss.

His master jumps
into the water
with his clothes on.

The king and
the princess come.

Puss says, Help, help!
The Marquis of Carrabas
is in the water.
Please come and help
my master!

The king's men help the boy.

They give the boy some good clothes.

Please come with me, says the king.

The boy gets into the carriage with the king and the princess.

Puss sees some men
working.

Here comes the king,
says Puss.
Please say you are
working for
the Marquis of Carrabas.

Yes, say the men.

The king comes.

He sees the men working.

We are working for
the Marquis of Carrabas,
say the men.

That is good,
says the king.

Puss comes
to an ogre's home.

He says, Can I come in?

Yes, says the ogre.
(The ogre wants
to eat Puss.)

Puss says to the ogre,
Can you change
into a lion?

Yes, says the ogre.

He changes into a lion.

That was good,
says Puss to the ogre.
Can you change
into a mouse?

Yes, says the ogre.
Look at me.

The ogre changes
into a mouse.

Puss jumps down.

He gets the mouse
and eats it.

The king comes.
This is my master's home,
says Puss.

Come in here and eat.

They go in and eat
the ogre's food.

Puss's master
likes the princess.

Please marry me,
he says.

Yes, says the princess.
I want to marry you.

The king is pleased.

Puss's master marries
the princess.

Puss is pleased.

He likes the princess
and the princess is good
to Puss.

LADYBIRD
READING SCHEMES

Read It Yourself links with all Ladybird reading schemes and can be used with any other method of learning to read.

Say the Sounds

Ladybird's **Say the Sounds** graded reading scheme is a *phonics* scheme. It teaches children the sounds of individual letters and letter combinations, enabling them to tackle new words by building them up as a blend of smaller units.

There are 8 titles in this scheme:

1 **Rocket to the jungle**
2 **Frog and the lollipops**
3 **The go-cart race**
4 **Pirate's treasure**
5 **Humpty Dumpty and the robots**
6 **Flying saucer**
7 **Dinosaur rescue**
8 **The accident**

Support material available: Practice Books, Double Cassette pack, Flash Cards